THE ADVENTURES OF PEANUT AND HECTOR: THE TWO BEARS MEET

by Whitney and John Matson,

Creators of Peanut and Hector, LLC

Illustrations by Conor Schultze

DORRANCE
PUBLISHING CO
EST. 1920
PITTSBURGH, PENNSYLVANIA 15238

Dorrance Publishing Co
585 Alpha Drive
Suite 103
Pittsburgh, PA 15238
Visit our website at *www.dorrancebookstore.com*

ISBN: 978-1-6376-4042-5
eISBN: 978-1-6376-4889-6

This book is dedicated to Brooks, Reagan, and London.

THE ADVENTURES OF PEANUT AND HECTOR: THE TWO BEARS MEET

THERE WAS A BIG BEAR, LIVING IN THE WOOD,

BOISTEROUS, BROWN AND BIG-BONED,

AND WHILE SHE CAME FROM A LARGE GRIZZLY FAMILY,

SHE FELT QUITE ALL ALONE.

HER PARENTS NAMED HER PEANUT,
AND HOPED FOR A REFINED LADY,
BUT SHE ATE HONEY WITH HER PAWS,
NAPPING ALL DAY IN TREES SHADY.

THE ANIMALS AT SCHOOL LAUGHED MEANLY,

WHEN PEANUT TRIED TO READ.

"I'LL NEVER FIT IN, I HAVE NO FRIENDS,

I FEEL LIKE SUCH A DWEEB."

THERE WAS ANOTHER BEAR AT THAT SCHOOL THERE,

WHO ALSO FELT LONELY AND SCARED,

HE WAS SMALL AND BLACK, SHARP AS A TACK,

AND FOR OTHERS HE DEEPLY CARED.

HIS PARENTS NAMED HIM HECTOR,
HOPING FOR A LARGE FIGHTING BRUTE,
BUT HECTOR WAS GENTLE, KIND TO OTHERS,
AND LOVED TO PLAY THE FLUTE!

ONE DAY AT RECESS, THERE WAS A BIG MESS,

INVOLVING HUGO THE HOUND.

HUGO MADE A GREAT SOUND, KNOCKED HECTOR DOWN,

AND PINNED HIM TO THE GROUND.

HECTOR WAS SHOCKED AND OFF-PUT,

CRYING AND FEELING FRIGHTFUL,

HE HEARD ALL THE KIDS THAT WERE LAUGHING,

AND NO LONGER FELT INSIGHTFUL.

PEANUT HAD WATCHED THIS WHOLE SCENE UNFOLD,

AND FELT DEEP DOWN INSIDE,

A RUMBLING GROWL, A RISING DRIVE,

TO HELP HECTOR THERE AS HE CRIED.

17

"ABSOLUTELY NOT!" SNARLED PEANUT HOT,

"YOU'LL BACK OFF RIGHT THIS INSTANT!"

HUGO COWERED LOW, AND WITHOUT A SHOW,

QUICKLY LET HECTOR GO.

SO THAT IS HOW THE SAGA BEGAN,

TWO BEARS WERE NOW UNITED.

FROM THAT DAY ON, THE BEARS WERE TOGETHER,

AND BOTH FELT DEEP-DOWN DELIGHTED.

CPSIA information can be obtained
at www.ICGtesting.com
Printed in the USA
LVRC100257231121
704189LV00001B/7